To Jackson & Collin Marley,
Enjoy!
Shane Durie

Here Comes Beso

By:
Shane Durie

Illustrations by:
Samantha Bantly

AuthorHouse™
1663 Liberty Drive
Bloomington, IN 47403
www.authorhouse.com
Phone: 1 (800) 839-8640

© 2017 Shane Durie. All rights reserved.

No part of this book may be reproduced, stored in a retrieval system,
or transmitted by any means without the written permission of the author.

Published by AuthorHouse 04/24/2017

ISBN: 978-1-5246-8904-9 (sc)
ISBN: 978-1-5246-8906-3 (hc)
ISBN: 978-1-5246-8905-6 (e)

Library of Congress Control Number: 2017906269

Print information available on the last page.

Any people depicted in stock imagery provided by Thinkstock are models,
and such images are being used for illustrative purposes only.
Certain stock imagery © Thinkstock.

This book is printed on acid-free paper.

Because of the dynamic nature of the Internet, any web addresses or links contained in this book may have changed since publication and may no longer be valid. The views expressed in this work are solely those of the author and do not necessarily reflect the views of the publisher, and the publisher hereby disclaims any responsibility for them.

authorHOUSE®

This is the story of a very special dog named Beso.

Beso has many friends and people who care for him.

But before I tell you all about Beso and his many friends, let's meet Beso.

First we have to find out where he is. Is he in the living room? No, but look on the sofa. There is Jordan laying down and there is Tigger napping on top of the sofa. They both live with Beso.

I bet Beso is outside. Let's take a look in the front yard.

I do not see him in the front yard. He must be in the back yard. Beso always comes running when you whistle. If you do not know how to whistle, clap your hands and call his name.

Here he comes! Here comes Beso! What a good boy.

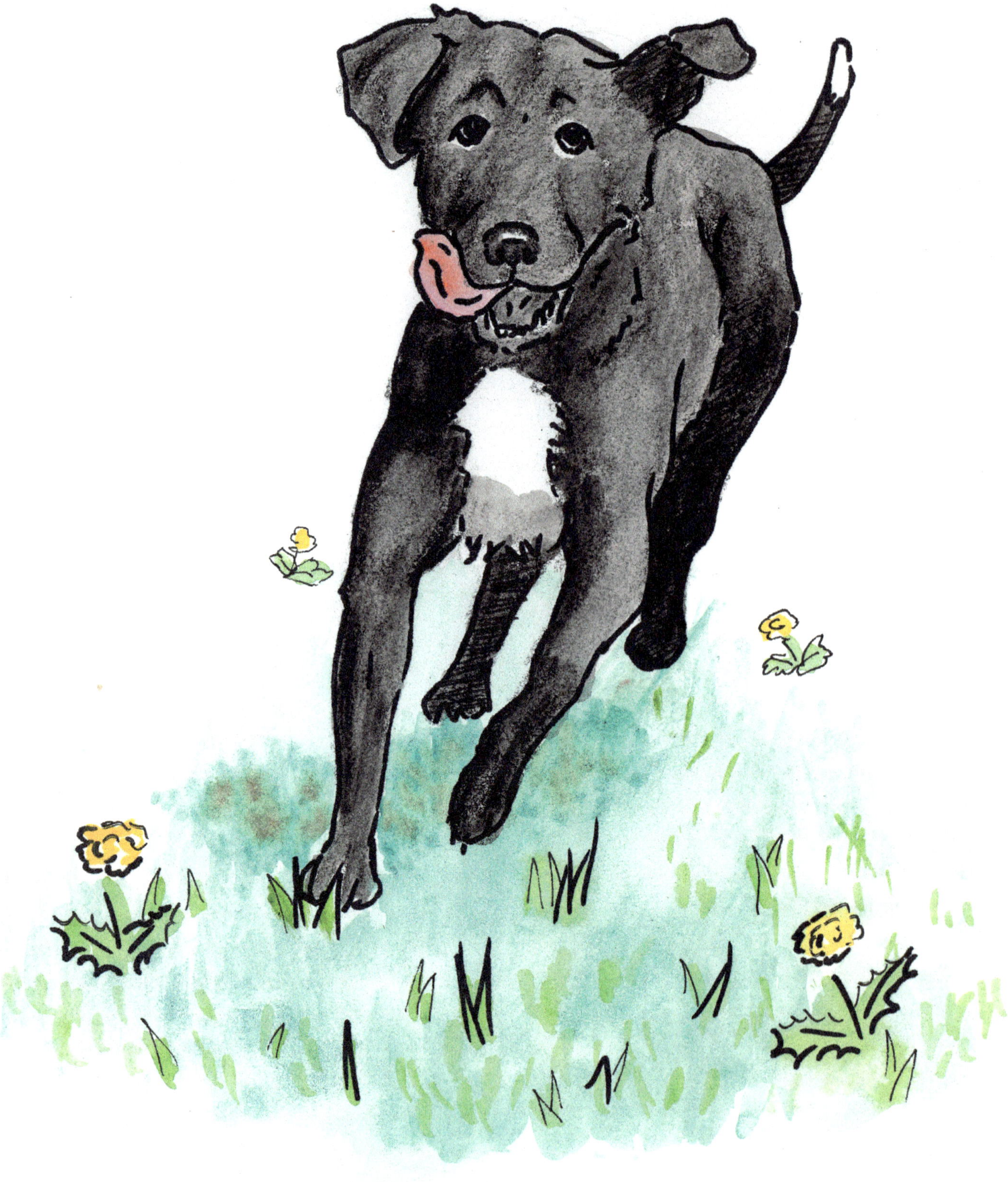

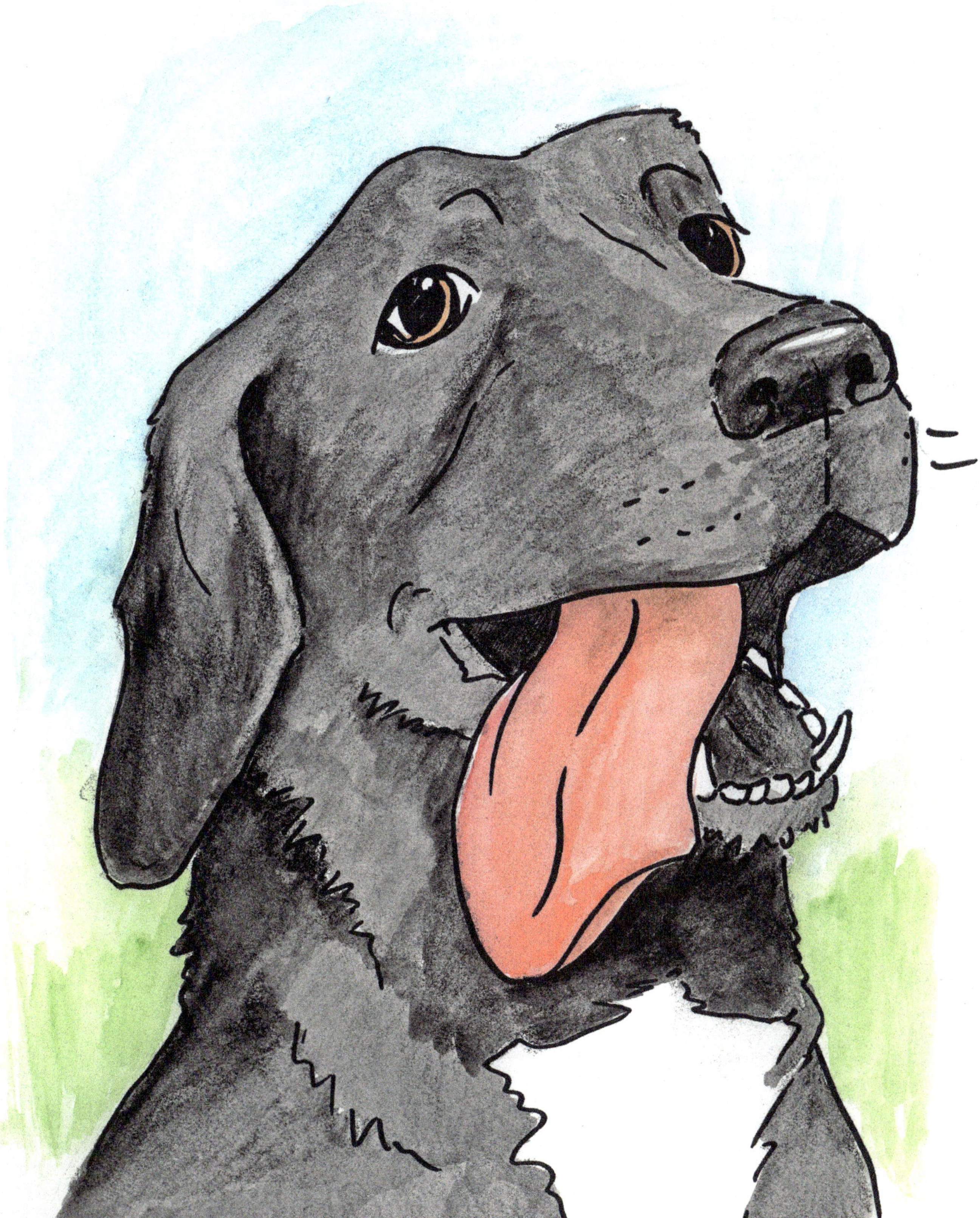

Beso lives a very happy life and has many adventures with his friends. Sometimes his adventures get him into trouble but he has people who care for him and take good care of him.

But Beso did not always have such a good life.
As a young puppy his life was very hard.

Beso was born in a big city and the first people who had him did not care for him or love him.

He was chained to a big oak tree in their front yard and was left alone all day and night.

A young lady walked by Beso on her way to school almost every day and noticed how sad he looked.

Many days it would be very hot and Beso did not have any water to cool him down.

Many nights on her way back home the lady would notice that Beso looked scared and lonely.

The lady decided that Beso should come live with her where he would get plenty of food and water.

But he would also get what all puppies need the most. That is love.

At first, Jordan was not very happy about Beso coming to live in her house but she learned to accept him and share her home with him. Tigger did not seem to mind at all.

Beso grew up to be a very happy dog and he is very grateful for his new life. Beso and the cats moved to a house in the country after the young lady finished school and it was here that Beso learned many things and met many new friends.

Beso is now a grown dog and he and the cats have lived together for many years. I would love to share some of Beso's adventures with you but we have come to the end of this book. Perhaps sometime soon I will write another book all about his exciting life. Until then, tell Beso goodbye.

CPSIA information can be obtained
at www.ICGtesting.com
Printed in the USA
BVOW05*0028050617
485706BV00004B/4/P

9 781524 689063